W9-BDW-010

A Jesse Steam Mystery

The Case of the Clicking Clock

Written & Illustrated by Ken Bowser

Solving Mysteries Through Science, Technology, Engineering, Art & Math

Egremont, Massachusetts

The Jesse Steam Mysteries are produced and published by:
Red Chair Press LLC PO Box 333 South Egremont, MA 01258-0333
www.redchairpress.com

 FREE Educator Guide at www.redchairpress.com/free-resources

For My Grandson, Liam

Publisher's Cataloging-In-Publication Data
Names: Bowser, Ken, author, illustrator.
Title: The case of the clicking clock / written & illustrated by Ken Bowser.

Description: South Egremont, MA : Red Chair Press, [2020] | Series: A Jesse Steam mystery | "Solving Mysteries Through Science, Technology, Engineering, Art & Math." | Includes a makerspace activity applying engineering skill to making a potato clock. | Summary: "A summer trip to her grandparents' house was going great until Jesse gets caught up in a mystery in the attic. When she encounters a pair of spooky, green eyes during a lightning storm, Jesse sets out to use engineering skills to solve the Case of the Clicking Clock"--Provided by publisher.

Identifiers: ISBN 9781634409452 (library hardcover) | ISBN 9781634409469 (paperback) | ISBN 9781634409476 (ebook)

Subjects: LCSH: Clocks and watches--Juvenile fiction. | Lightning--Juvenile fiction. | Engineering--Juvenile fiction. | CYAC: Clocks and watches--Fiction. | Lightning--Fiction. | Engineering--Fiction. | LCGFT: Detective and mystery fiction.

Classification: LCC PZ7.B697 Ca 2020 (print) | LCC PZ7.B697 (ebook) | DDC [Fic]--dc23

LC record available at https://lccn.loc.gov/2019936019

Printed in the United States of America

0520 1P CGF20

Table of Contents

Cast of Characters

Jesse Steam

Amateur sleuth and all-around neat kid. Jesse loves riding her bike, solving mysteries, and most of all, Mr. Stubbs. Jesse is never without her messenger bag and the cool stuff it holds.

Mr. Stubbs

A cat with an attitude, he's the coolest tabby cat in Deanville. Stubbs was a stray cat who strayed right into Jesse's heart. Can you figure out how he got his name?

Professor Peach

A retired university professor. Professor Peach knows tons of cool stuff and is somewhat of a legend in Deanville. He has college degrees in Science, Technology, Engineering, Art and Math.

Emmett

Professor Peach's ever-present pet, white lab rat. He loves cheese balls, and wherever you find The Professor, you're sure to find Emmett—even though he might be difficult to spot!

Clark & Lewis

Jesse's next-door neighbor and sometimes formidable adversary, Clark Johnson, and his slippery, slimy, gross-looking pet frog, Lewis. Yuck.

Dorky Dougy

Clark Johnson's three-year-old, tag-along baby brother. Dougy is never without his stuffed alligator, a rubber knife, and something really goofy to say, like "eleventy-seven."

Kimmy Kat Black

Holder of the Deanville Elementary School Long Jump Record, know-it-all, and self-proclaimed future member of Mensa. Kimmy Kat Black lives near the Spooky Tree.

Liam LePoole

A black belt in karate, and also the captain of the Deanville Community Swimming Pool Cannonball Team. Liam's best friend is Chompy Dog, his stinky, gassy, and frenzied brown Puggle.

Lolly

Jesse's feisty grandmother and admitted "cat lady". Lolly is an avid ukulele player, and she always seems to smell like freshly baked chocolate chip cookies.

Poppie

Jesse's sweet grandfather. He is an avid bowler, fisherman, and the owner of the world's largest collection of suspenders, black knee socks, and bow ties.

The Town of Deanville

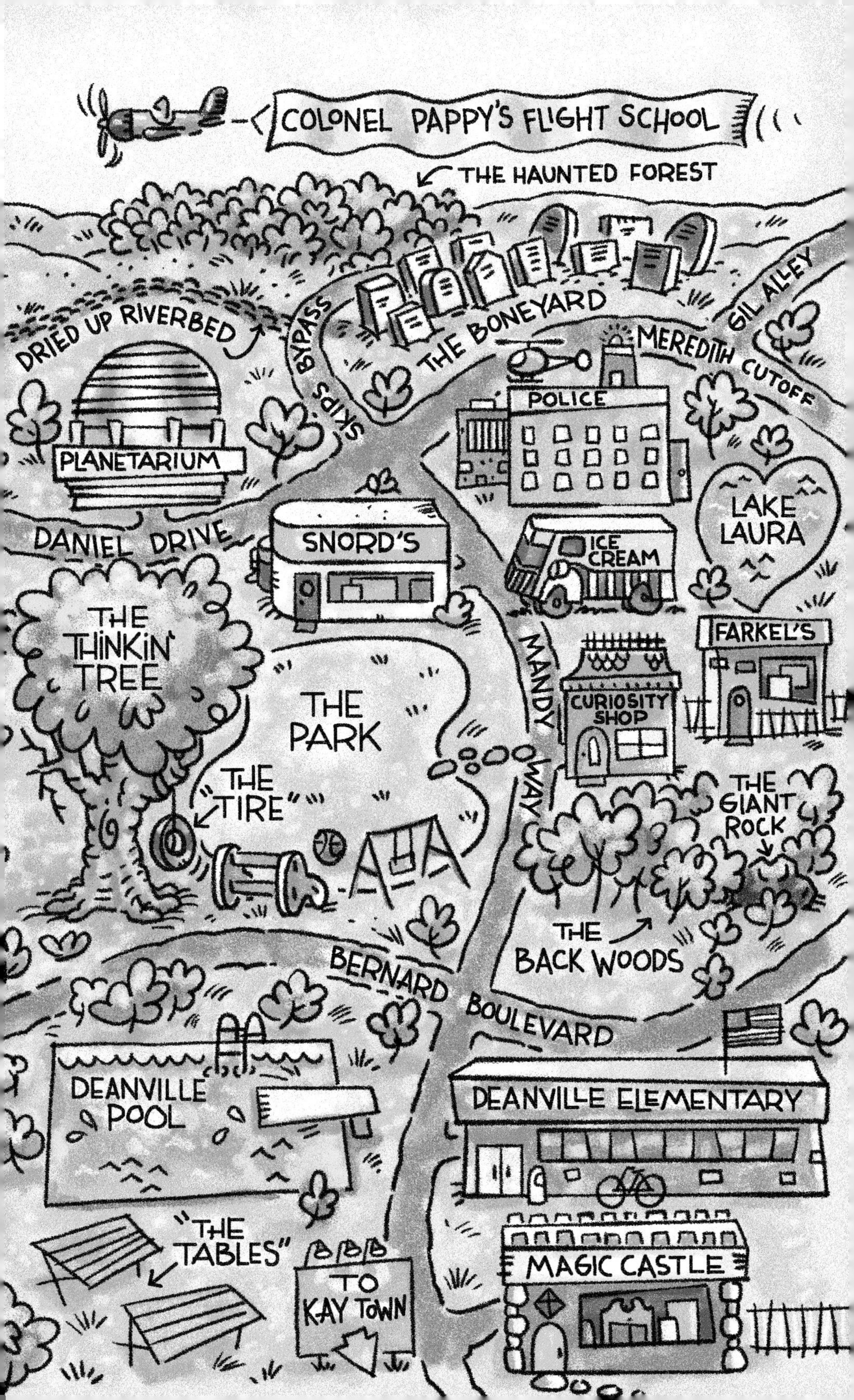
COLONEL PAPPY'S FLIGHT SCHOOL
THE HAUNTED FOREST
THE BONEYARD
GIL ALLEY
MEREDITH CUTOFF
DRIED UP RIVERBED
SKIPS BYPASS
PLANETARIUM
POLICE
LAKE LAURA
DANIEL DRIVE
SNORD'S
ICE CREAM
FARKEL'S
THE THINKIN' TREE
THE PARK
MANDY WAY
CURIOSITY SHOP
"THE TIRE"
THE GIANT ROCK
THE BACK WOODS
BERNARD BOULEVARD
DEANVILLE POOL
DEANVILLE ELEMENTARY
"THE TABLES"
TO KAY TOWN
MAGIC CASTLE

Bees and Bats and Snoozing Cats

Chapter 1

BUZZ! BUZZ! BUZZ! Jesse turned her head just in time to see the enormous swarm of killer bees that were circling her by the thousands upon thousands. *BUZZ! BUZZ! BUZZ!* The horde came closer and closer, and the deafening sound of the swarm grew louder and louder in Jesse's ringing ears. *BUZZ! BUZZ! BUZZ!* The swarm began to close in on Jesse's face, and she could feel the wind created by millions of tiny beating wings across her cheeks! Trying to run, it seemed like her feet would just not move, as if she were wearing two giant, 100-pound boots. *Oh no,* she thought. *Help!* She tried to yell, but all that came out of her mouth was a muffled "arrgghh!" The throng grew nearer. The buzzing grew louder. She felt tiny insect feet as they landed on her nose!

Snort. Gasp. Cough. “Huh? What?” Jesse mumbled from a sleepy daze. “What’s going on?” She blinked her eyes open, only to find Mr. Stubbs licking her cheek, his whiskers tickling her nose like tiny bee feet. “Oh. Stubbs. It’s you.” She yawned.

BUZZ! BUZZ! BUZZ! Jesse’s alarm clock blared loudly. *BUZZ! BUZZ! BUZZ!* It went off again. Jesse sat up and swatted the button on the top of the alarm clock to stop its complaining, but that didn’t work. She swatted again—still no luck. Fumbling, Jesse reached the clock’s electrical cord and yanked it from the wall to stop the constant *buzz, buzz, buzz*ing. Finally. Silence.

“Oh man,” she said to Stubbs as she sat up further in bed. “What a bizarre dream *that* was,” she said, rubbing her eyes.

It was a warm summer morning, and Jesse had set her alarm for 6:00 am. “We want to make sure we catch the sunrise, Stubbs!”

STUBBS
6:00

Settling into the wicker chair on her front porch, Jesse prepared to watch the sun lift the curtain on a new day. A few crickets chirped. A shooting star scratched a paper-thin line through the early morning darkness, and she heard the faint bark of a dog far off in the quiet distance.

"Isn't this your favorite time of the day?" Jesse asked Mr. Stubbs, who was already back asleep on Jesse's lap. "It's so tranquil. Stubbs. Are you awake?" She giggled.

A pair of bats fluttered by, darting back and forth for their early breakfast of tiny morning insects. "Do bats eat bees?" Jesse asked the sleeping kitty with a chuckle.

Time Flies and Then It Doesn't

Chapter 2

The sun broke over the horizon, the stars faded away, and the bats fluttered back to their bat houses with full bat bellies.

"Ya know, Stubbs..." Jesse poked the snoozing cat's tummy. "It's glorious summer mornings like this that make each and every day extra special." She sighed.

"We're visiting Lolly and Poppie tomorrow, and we'll all be able to catch a few beautiful sunrises together," she went on. "You know how early my grandparents like to get up every morning!" Jesse laughed.

"I can hear Poppie now." She smiled at the still-sleeping Mr. Stubbs. " 'There's a sunrise and a sunset every single day.' " Jesse mimicked her grandfather in a funny, deep voice. " 'And they're absolutely free!' " She chuckled as she went on with her impression.

After breakfast, Jesse went back up to her room and began to pack for the trip. She and her family visited her grandparents for a few days every summer, and this year was no exception. “I can hardly wait to see them again this year,” Jesse said to Stubbs, who was already back asleep.

“I just love exploring their old farmhouse and looking at all of the neat old things they have,” she continued.

Jesse began to set out all of the items that she wanted to bring with her in her messenger bag. “Can’t forget my spyglass,” she said out loud to Stubbs. “Or my journal.” Jesse rarely went anywhere without her tools—especially her journal. “You never know when you’re going to run into a new mystery to solve, Stubby boy,” she said.

“I’ll bring a measuring tape and a pocket calculator just in case I need them,” she said. “A flashlight is always good to have handy too. Oh, and I can’t forget my watch.”

Finished with her packing, Jesse set her suitcase and messenger bag out right next to her bedroom door.

"Okay. We're all ready for tomorrow, Stubby, old boy. Now, remember, we're leaving for Lolly and Poppie's first thing in the morning," she reminded Mr. Stubbs. "So let's make sure we're up and ready!"

Just as Jesse was finished packing, she heard a familiar voice at her window. "JESSE!" the voice scolded firmly. "Where have you been? We were supposed to meet up at the park an hour ago. Remember?"

It was Kimmy Kat Black, and she was not the least bit happy. "Oh my gosh," Jesse said. "Is it three o'clock already?" Jesse glanced at the watch on her wrist.

"Stopped? I'm sorry, Kimmy. It looks like I forgot to put my watch on the charger again," she apologized.

"That's okay," Kimmy replied. "We still have time to hang out before your trip tomorrow."

Jesse and Kimmy hung out in the park for the rest of the day. The whole gang was there. Clark was there with his pet frog Lewis. Clark's little brother Dougy was there, of course, and so was Liam LePoole with his stinky mutt Chompy Dog.

"Chompy Dog is cool, but boy, does he have bad breath," Clark Johnson said as he made a scrunched-up face.

"He also has a serious drooling problem," Kimmy Kat Black said as she took a step back from Chompy Dog.

The kids were still laughing when they heard a long "Fffrrrrrrttt" sound.

"What was that?" Clark laughed.

"Man, Liam! Your dog just tooted!" said Kimmy.

"Ewww! Your dog is flatulent, Liam!" Clark laughed.

"Yeah! Your dog is flap-a-champ!" Dorky Dougy said.

"Not a word, Dougy!" They all laughed.

Just then the big town clock struck seven. "Yikes! Gotta run!" Jesse yelled back at her friends as she took off. "I was supposed to be home for dinner an hour ago!"

Over the River and Through the Woods

Chapter 3

Bam, bam, bam! "Huh? What?" Jesse jerked from her sleep. *Bam, bam, bam!* Startled, Mr. Stubbs jumped and darted beneath the bed.

"JESSE! We're leaving here in five minutes!" Jesse's dad pounded from outside of her bedroom door. "You hear me? Five minutes!"

Jesse sat up, rubbed her eyes, and looked over at her way-too-silent alarm clock.

"Oh no!" she yelled to Stubbs, who was peeking out from under the bed. "We overslept! I forgot to plug that darn clock back in from yesterday!" She moaned. "What is it with me and clocks these days?"

Scrambling to her feet, Jesse called out to Stubbs. "C'mon, dude. We gotta hurry." She grabbed Stubbs, her watch, and her two bags and headed for the door.

From the back seat of the car, Jesse could see the sun beginning to peek out from behind the trees, just as it did on the mornings she sat in her porch chair watching the day begin.

"Not that many bats out this morning, Stubbs," she said to the cat that was once again sound asleep, his head on her lap.

It was a long four-hour drive to her grandparents' house in Kyleville, and as they drove they passed the Deanville Bank, with its digital clock that spelled out the time with bright illuminated numbers rather than traditional clock hands, *6:23,* it read.

After a while they drove past the big town clock that had struck 7:00 the night before.

"Don't ya just love that big, beautiful ol' clock, Stubbs?" Jesse quizzed the snoring cat. "I wonder who's in charge of making sure that thing's plugged in every night?" She giggled to Stubbs as he snoozed.

DEANVILLE
ANVILLE
ATIONAL
BANK
5:23

The morning clicked by and Mr. Stubbs continued to snooze on Jesse's lap.

"I wonder what the gang is up to right about now?" Jesse asked Stubbs as he carried on with his cat nap. "No idea, huh, dude?" She nudged him again.

The car rocked back and forth as they drove. Jesse removed her journal from her messenger bag and began to make a few entries. "I like to keep a good record of the day's events," she would often say.

She glanced down at her wristwatch as she began to write.

"9:42 am, August 31st," she began her entry. "We're on the way to my grandparents' house. Just like last summer, we are headed for a two-day visit," she continued to write. "We've been driving for almost four hours, and I'm looking forward to seeing Lolly and Poppie and exploring their cool old farmhouse. And Mr. Stubbs is still asleep—

nothing new there," she continued to jot in her journal. "And I'm beginning to get a bit drowsy myself..."

Cobwebs, Spiders and the Smell of Gross Underwear

Chapter 4

COO-coo. COO-coo. COO-coo.

"It's three o'clock, Stubbs," Jesse said. "Time to wake up from your fourth afternoon nap of the day, you lazy critter."

Jesse knew the time from the sound of her grandmother's cuckoo clock downstairs in the kitchen.

"We've been here at my grandparents' house for five hours now, Stubby, old boy. I've had lunch, unpacked, organized all of my things, and I've written four pages in my journal. All you've managed to accomplish is four consecutive naps, cuckoo cat."

"I think it's about time we head out and poke around a bit, old chum," she said to Mr. Stubbs. Jesse checked her watch again. "We have three hours before we have to be back here for dinner."

Jesse grabbed her messenger bag as she and Mr. Stubbs headed down the long winding staircase that led to the kitchen.

"There's the old cuckoo clock," she said to Stubbs, pointing it out. "Lolly and Poppie brought that back with them a long, long time ago from their trip to Germany."

As they passed the clock, Jesse saw something she had not noticed before—a doorway.

"Gee, I wonder where this goes?" she whispered to Stubbs. Jesse grabbed the doorknob and turned it slowly. The old stone knob was cold in her hand, and the door opened with a long *skaweeeeeeeek*.

"It sure is dark down there," Jesse murmured to Stubbs as she peered down the dark, open staircase with her flashlight.

Mr. Stubbs hid behind Jesse's leg, not wanting to go any further. "C'mon, scaredy-cat. What do *you* have to be afraid of?"

The stair let out a wooden squeak as Jesse took the first step down into the dark, silent stairwell.

"It sure is cold and dank down here," Jesse whispered to Stubbs, who clung closely to her leg. "And this railing sure is wobbly."

Jesse felt something sticky and tickly on her nose. "Phhht!" She let out a spitty noise.

"Cobwebs!" she shrieked. "I hate cobwebs." She batted aimlessly at her face in the darkness.

"I sure hope there are no spiders down here. If there's one thing I hate more than

cobwebs, it's spiders. And where there are cobwebs, there are usually spiders," she worried aloud to Stubbs.

The next step squeaked even louder than the last one. Jesse moved slowly down the dark wooden stairs, her flashlight moving up and down and side to side, trying its hardest to light the way, one small spot at a time. "Sure is a long way down here," she said.

Reaching the bottom of the stairs, Jesse could tell that she was now standing on a hard stone floor.

"What is that gross smell?" she asked Stubbs. "It smells like a pile of nasty, sweaty, old underwear down here."

The two stared at the spot that Jesse's flashlight created as it moved across the dark, eerie walls of the musty basement.

"No spiders so far," Jesse said. She moved her flashlight again, this time deeper into the back of the dark, windowless basement.

"Stubbs? Where are you?" Jesse called.

Jesse looked up to see a tall, shadowy figure coming toward her. "Wha... wha... what is that?!" she yelled to Stubbs, but Stubbs was nowhere to be found.

Taking a step back, Jesse fell, sending her flashlight spinning across the floor as the shadowy figure lurched forward and landed right on top of her. "Ahhhh!" she screamed.

Jesse scrambled across the floor on her hands and knees for her flashlight. She backed up against the cold basement wall

and pointed the light toward the shadowy figure that lay still on the ground.

Jesse poked the motionless thing with her flashlight. Nothing. She nudged it with her shoe. Still nothing. Slowly, she rolled it over.

"A dressmaker's mannequin!" Jesse laughed. "Stubbs, you scared me half to death when you knocked that thing over on top of me!"

Jesse brushed herself off. "I've had enough fun for one afternoon," she said to Stubbs. "Let's head back upstairs."

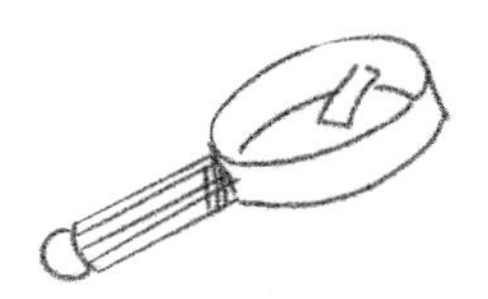

An Electrical Storm and a Pair of Shifty Green Eyes

Chapter 5

Jesse finished her dinner while Mr. Stubbs polished off the last of his kibble from the kitty food bowl beneath Jesse's chair.

"As soon as we're done cleaning up these dishes we can go explore some more, Stubbs," she said to the munching cat. "But you need to stick right by my side the entire time," she scolded him. "I don't want a repeat of this afternoon when you wandered off, knocked that mannequin down on top of me, and nearly scared me half to death." She laughed as she picked up her dinner plate.

"I saw another mysterious doorway this morning. It looked like it might go up to the attic. Maybe we can poke around up there."

After drying off the last of the dinner plates, Jesse sat down and made a few entries into her journal:

"August 31st. 6:42 pm. Got caught up in a tangle of cobwebs today. Gross! I HATE cobwebs *and* spiders!" she scrawled.

"Then, thanks to old Stubby boy, I was attacked by a dressmaker's mannequin," the note went on. "I just about fainted!" She ended with a huge exclamation mark.

Then Jesse made one last entry into her journal: "Now Stubbs and I are headed into the attic to see what's up there. I just hope there are no cobwebs—or surprises," she ended the note.

Jesse closed her journal and grabbed her bag. "Never know what ya might need when you go exploring." She motioned to Stubbs. "Let's go, dude," she said as she flicked on her flashlight.

The door to the attic was very slender—much more narrow than a regular door, like

the one that led down the basement stairs. The stairs themselves were very steep and seemed to go almost straight up. The sides of the stairway were not open like the stairs that led down into the basement. Rather, they were closed in, making the entire space seem really confining.

With a click, Jesse flipped the wall switch just inside the door, and a dim, yellow bulb tried its best to illuminate the top of the stairs.

"Well, that doesn't do much good, now, does it, Stubbs?" Jesse said. "We're still going to need our flashlight if we're going to see anything."

Stubbs cowered behind Jesse's leg, just as he had done earlier that day in the basement. The air grew very still, and Jesse could hear thunder from a distant storm.

The two explorers began their slow climb up the dark, claustrophobic stairs. "You right behind me, Stubbs?" Jesse whispered as she climbed. Stubbs let out a meek little mew.

Another step and then another. Thirteen steps in all and they found themselves at the top of the staircase, peering into the open attic.

"Whooooa," Jesse whispered. "Look at those giant rafters."

Jesse shined her flashlight at the top of the attic. The ceiling was tall and pointy in the middle, but it sloped down sharply as it met the floorboards on either side. "Those

beams must be a foot thick," she marveled in a low whisper. "I'll bet they're a hundred years old."

Jesse and Stubbs moved further into the dark attic. Faint moonlight shined dimly in through two eye-shaped windows at the far end of the attic. Jesse could hear the buzz of the electric wires in the walls and the sound of a radio playing in the downstairs den. She

could also hear the rumble of that distant storm, but this time it was much closer.

Suddenly, a loud *CRACK* split the night! The room went completely dark and silent.

"The storm must have knocked the power out," Jesse whispered to Stubbs, who was

hiding behind her again. The attic was so quiet Jesse could hear her own pulse beating.

"What's that sound?" she whispered again to Stubbs. "Listen."

Tick. Tock. Tick. Tock. Tick. Tock.

The dark attic was now in complete silence, except for a slow, rhythmic *Tick. Tock. Tick. Tock. Tick. Tock.* "That almost sounds like a heartbeat." Jesse shivered as she whispered to Stubbs.

Shining her flashlight toward the sound, Jesse witnessed two big green eyes moving back and forth rhythmically with the sound. *Tick. Tock,* the sound went. *Tick. Tock.* The eyes moved.

Jesse lowered her flashlight slightly, only to reveal a sinister grin with flashing teeth, below the shifting green eyes.

"Yikes!" Jesse dropped her flashlight.

Jesse retrieved her flashlight, and she and Stubbs took a few slow steps back.

"Why, it's just an old grandfather clock," Jesse said with a delighted smile, as she lit up the entire thing with her flashlight.

Jesse was amazed at the carved wooden clock and at the old clock's face with its intricate dials and hands. "Look at this, Stubbs," she said. "These dials show the phases of the moon, and the sun, and the Earth."

The eyes continued to move back and forth with every tick and every tock.

"But I don't get it," she went on to Stubbs. "The power is out to the entire house. How in the world is this thing still running?" she asked the puzzled cat. "It's too old for batteries or a charger."

"Another mystery," she sighed.

Another Day, Another Mystery

Chapter 6

Back home from their trip, the sun rose over Jesse's front porch precisely at 6:57 am, according to Jesse's wristwatch, just as it had before her visit to her grandparents' house.

"What do you want to do this fine summer day, Stubby, old boy?" she asked the snoring cat. If there was one special talent that Mr. Stubbs possessed, it was the art of snoozing.

"I'll tell you what I'd like to do," she continued. "I'd like to somehow figure out how that beautiful old grandfather clock kept right on working, while everything else in Lolly and Poppie's house stopped dead while the power was out." Jesse poked the sleeping cat on his belly. "And I know just who to ask." She winked.

Jesse plopped Mr. Stubbs into the basket on the front of her bike and started out for Professor Peach's house next door. "The Professor has college degrees in science, technology, engineering, art, and math," Jesse told Mr. Stubbs. "If anyone can solve the mystery of the clicking clock, it's him."

"Hey, Jesse, wait up!" Jesse heard a voice call out as she pedaled her bike toward the Professor's front porch. It was Kimmy Kat Black, along with the rest of the gang.

"Where ya going?" Kimmy asked.

"Over to Professor Peach's house," Jesse replied. "I saw a cool old clock at my grandparents' house over the weekend. A storm knocked the power out to the entire house, but the old clock kept on running," she explained. "I can't figure out how and thought that if anyone could explain it, the Professor could."

STUB

"Hey, why don't you all go with me?" Jesse asked the kids.

"Sounds fun to me," Liam LePoole chimed in. "I always love a good mystery."

Clark Johnson spoke up. "Yes, a puzzling enigma is always interesting," Clark spouted off.

"Yeah, I like a good a-meeg-na," Clark's little brother Dougy repeated.

"Not a word, Dougy!" The gang laughed.

As the group approached the Professor's house, they found him standing out on his front porch.

"Hi, Professor!" the kids called out.

"Well, what do we have here?" the Professor called back with a grin.

Harmonic
What, What,
What?

Chapter 7

Jesse told Professor Peach all about her trip to her grandparents' house and all about the beautiful old grandfather clock, as the other kids looked on with fascination.

"The power was out to the entire house," she recounted. "But the old clock kept on ticking. I know it's too old to use batteries or a charger," she told the Professor. "So, how did it keep working?"

"Ah, Jesse, my dear. You are the curious one, aren't you?" The Professor smiled.

"You are correct," the Professor professed. "Those types of clocks came along well before there were batteries or electricity," he went on.

"That old clock is operated by gravity, along with what we refer to as *harmonic oscillation*," he explained.

“Harmonic what, what, what?” Jesse asked with a puzzled look on her face.

The Professor talked as he drew on a whiteboard. “That clock does not need

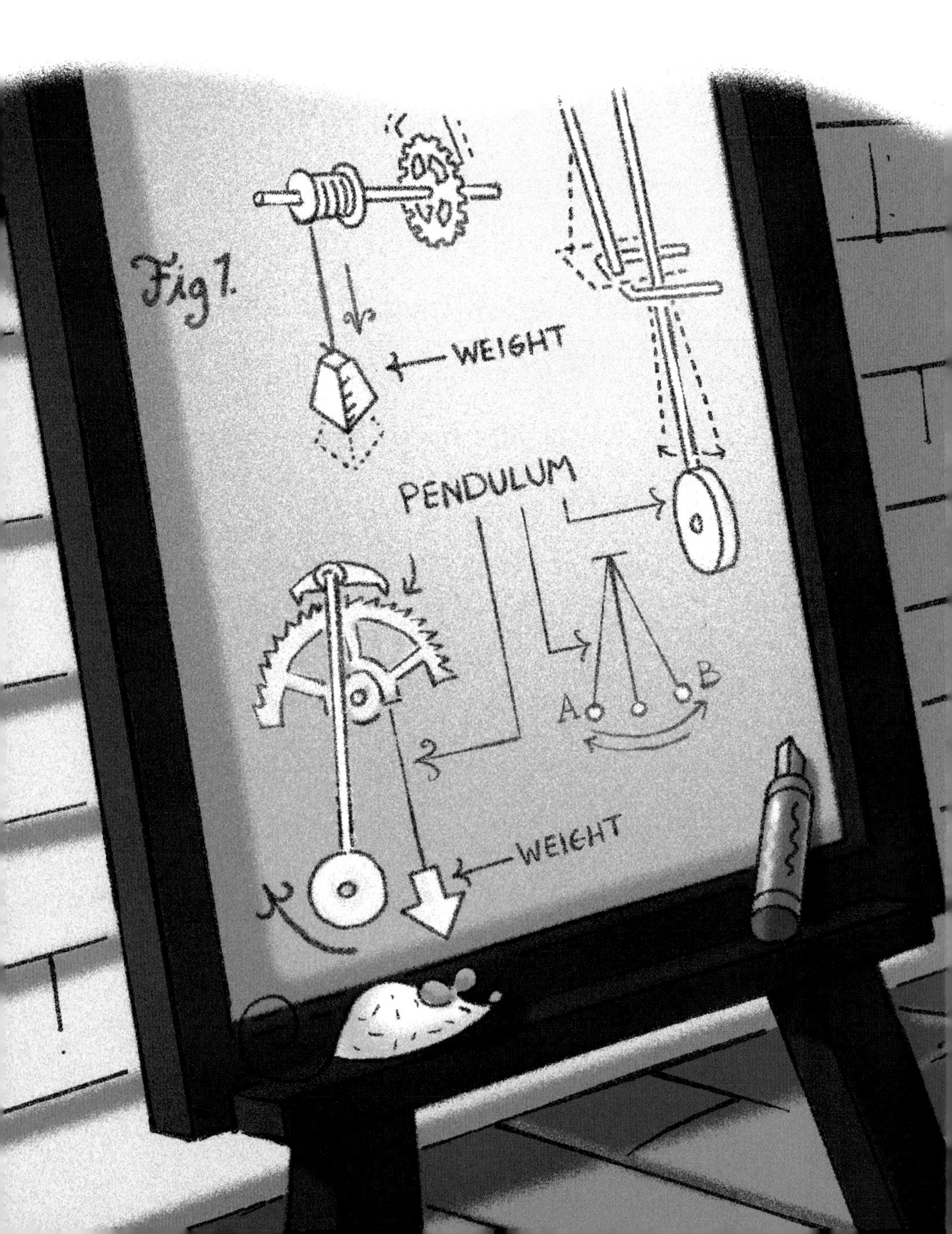

batteries or electricity to keep going because it uses the forces of nature. These weights," he pointed out, "store potential energy and release it to the clock mechanism as they fall, while a pendulum *oscillates* back and forth to regulate the clock's speed. Let me explain further."

The Professor created a diagram of the inside of the clock, along with notes and arrows.

"You see," he said, "the weights drop slowly over the course of hours or days, causing the gears to revolve, which in turn cause the hands of the clock to advance. The steady oscillation of the pendulum moves the gears at the correct speed. The gears also work the clock's other movements, like its eyes, dials, and chimes. The only other thing required to keep the clock ticking is for someone—like your grandfather, Jesse—to come along every so often to raise the weights back up, giving them more stored energy. Otherwise," he explained, "the clock would simply stop. You see, kids, with the mechanism inside the clock, we've harnessed the forces of nature as a tool to help us keep track of time."

"Whoa," the kids whispered in unison.

The Professor went on to describe other types of timekeeping devices that utilize the forces of nature.

"A sundial," the Professor spoke as he drew on the board, "uses the sun itself to help us track the hours of the day. While with an hourglass, we measure the passing of time by how long it takes for sand to go from the top of the glass to the bottom."

With this, the Professor held up a beautiful old hourglass.

"Then there were ancient clocks that were powered by falling water," he continued.

"In fact..." The Professor grinned with a twinkle in his eye. "I can even show you how we can use an ordinary potato from the supermarket to power one of today's simple digital clocks."

"A potato clock!" The kids all laughed.

"That's right." The Professor smiled. "Let me show you how..."

THE END

Jesse's Word List

Bizarre
strange—like your neighbor's blue hair

Claustrophobic
how you feel in a tight space—like under your bed

Consecutive
happening in a row—*He burped fourteen consecutive times.*

Dank
rhymes with stank—damp and stinky, like your gross, old gym socks

Drowsy
feeling really sleepy—like in math class

Enigma
totally mysterious—like algebra

Enormous
really, really, really, really, really big

Flatulent
to have gas—*Coach Bob was flatulent.*

Intricate
detailed—*The stain on his shirt was intricate.*

Mannequin
a big dummy, but not the human kind

Mimic
to imitate someone—like when you make fun of your teacher's voice

Musty
just like dank, but spelled differently

Oscillate
to move back and forth like a tire swing

Scaredy-cat
a timid person—*The new kid was a scaredy-cat because he was the new kid.*

Scrawl
to scribble words or letters—*The teacher scrawled an F on my book report.*

About the Author & Illustrator

Ken Bowser is an illustrator and writer whose work has appeared in hundreds of books and countless periodicals. While he's been drawing for as long as he could hold a pencil, all of his work today is created digitally on a computer. He works out of his home studio in Central Florida with his wife Laura and a big, lazy, orange cat.

Try It Out!

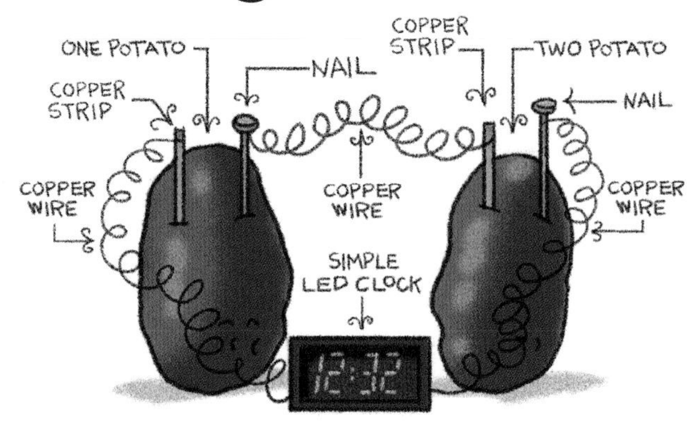

How to Make a Potato Clock

Making a clock run on potato power is easier than you think!

What You Need: Two potatoes, two pieces of heavy copper strips, two galvanized nails, thin copper wire, and one simple low-voltage LED clock.

Steps:

1. Remove the battery from the clock. Make a note of the positive (+) and negative (-) points of the battery.
2. Number the potatoes as 1 and 2. Insert one nail in each potato. Then insert one heavy copper strip into each potato, away from the nail.
3. Connect the wire in potato 1 to the positive (+) terminal in the clock. Then connect the nail in potato 2 to the negative (-) terminal in the clock.
4. Connect the nail in potato 1 to the copper wire in potato 2.

The potato battery is now an electrochemical battery. Chemical energy is converted to electric energy by electron transfer. In the case of the potato, the zinc in the nail reacts with the copper wire. Electron transfer takes place over the copper wires of the circuit, which channels the energy into the clock. You've harnessed potato power!